TAV/CH

the world's GREATEST underachiever

Hank ZipZER

**Hank Zipzer the World's
Greatest Underachiever series
by Henry Winkler and Lin Oliver**

the world's GREATEST underachiever

HankZ!pzER

THE COW POO TREASURE HUNT

THEO BAKER

WALKER
ENTERTAINMENT

This is a work of fiction. Names, characters, places and incidents are either
the product of the author's imagination or, if real, used fictitiously.
All statements, activities, stunts, descriptions, information and material
of any other kind contained herein are included for entertainment purposes only
and should not be relied on for accuracy or replicated as they may result in injury.

First published in Great Britain 2015 by Walker Entertainment,
an imprint of Walker Books Ltd, 87 Vauxhall Walk, London SE11 5HJ

Based on the television series "Hank Zipzer"
produced by Kindle Entertainment
in association with DHX Media Ltd.
Based on the screenplay *The Cow Poo Treasure Hunt*.
Reproductions © 2014 Hank Zipzer Productions Limited

2 4 6 8 10 9 7 5 3 1

Text © 2015 Walker Books Ltd
Cover by Walker Books Ltd

This book has been typeset in OpenDyslexic

Printed and bound in Great Britain by Clays Ltd, St Ives plc

British Library Cataloguing in Publication Data:
a catalogue record for this book is available from the British Library

ISBN 978-1-4063-5972-5

www.walker.co.uk

This book has been set in OpenDyslexic –
a font which has been created
to increase readability for readers
with dyslexia. The font is continually
being updated and improved,
based on input from dyslexic users.

CHAPTER ONE

I wanted to puke. I mean, I didn't really
want to puke. No one *wants* to puke. Not
even those hot-dog-eating champions
who chow down sixty hot dogs in ten
minutes. I bet their stomachs want to hurl,
though. My stomach definitely did – but it
was empty. I hadn't eaten anything since
breakfast, and all I'd had then was a glass
of orange juice. And that was eighteen
hours ago. Or was it twenty? Or was it ...
a lifetime ago?

I was a different man then.

I was Old Hank.

New Hank had seen things. Things too terrible to mention at the beginning of a book.

New Hank had *done* things too. Shameful things. New Hank had crippled an innocent badger – possibly.

And at this very moment, New Hank was on his hands and knees in the mud, rummaging through cowpats. In the middle of the night. With McKelty.

"I'm going to puke," I said.

"Stop saying that, Zitzer! Not one more word," said McKelty.

"I'm serious. I can feel chunks moving up my throat."

"You better swallow them. If you vomit, then I will, and McKeltys *do not* vomit. Ever."

"What's the matter, McKelty?" I asked. "Are you afraid of a little sick?"

"I fear nothing."

In the distance, beyond the steaming field of cowpats, an animal howled into the night.

"It's getting closer," McKelty whispered.

We were silent as we considered this fact. Then we heard thunder rumbling.

"You know what, McSmelty?" I said. "I think we're bonding."

"I'm not talking to you any more."

"I mean it," I said. "We're becoming friends. You're OK, McKelty, you really are."

I heard those words coming out of my mouth — but could I really think that? Was I telling the truth? McKelty was Champion Jerk of the Universe, and he'd teased and tried to sabotage me at least 3.4 million times, and that was just this week. Could it be that I was starting to *like* him?

I was so confused. But I guessed that was only natural. After you've been crawling through cowpats and touching them with both hands for more than forty minutes, things tend to get a bit confusing.

9

But this was more than confusing. This was a nightmare!

There was another roll of thunder.

Was this really happening? Was I really on my hands and knees in a muddy field, miles and miles from the nearest drainage system and/or falafel stand? Was I about to be electrocuted by lightning? Were those really my hands poking through cowpats?

No, I wasn't dreaming. You don't smell cowpats in your dreams. This was for real. This was as real as it gets.

This was a little *too* real.

I tried to remember what had brought me to this low point. But things weren't really connecting in my head. I wasn't thinking clearly. I remembered reading somewhere that sniffing too many cowpats can make you a little loopy. Or maybe I'd been sniffing cowpat fumes for so long that I was making up memories?

In my cowpat stupor, I started to see

flashes of my old life. Waking up in a soft bed. Drinking orange juice for breakfast. Petting friendly dogs. Running water coming out of a tap. Walking down a clean hallway.

Ah, there's Old Hank now, just hanging out with his two best mates in the world... What were their names again? Frankie and ... Ashley. That was it. Just look at Old Hank. He's such a happy, clean boy. So smiling and carefree. Sure, he's got small, childish concerns. Old Hank wants to go to the shopping centre with his friends...

No, I tell him. *It isn't worth it, Old Hank. Stay at home. Do not under any circumstances—*

A crash of thunder snapped me back to reality. It had started to rain. I shook my fist at the terrible sky and tried, with all my might, to scream, but the only thing that came out of my mouth was partially digested orange juice...

CHAPTER TWO

Three days earlier...

"This Saturday, Hank, are you in?" my best friend, Frankie, asked as we headed to class. "Hank?"

I didn't answer immediately because I was looking out of the window. Bill the school caretaker was trying to catch a stray cat that had wandered into the playground. It was a cute orange cat, with brown stripes, a white tuft of chest fur and a crooked white moustache. Bill had cornered the poor guy, but Alnor — my name for the cat, by the way — wasn't going quietly. They'd settled into stalemate. Bill had the broom, and Alnor the Orange had his claws. Bill would poke at Alnor with the broom; Alnor would hiss at the broom. Bill would jump back; Alnor would jump back. Then they'd have a stare-down. Then Bill would take another swipe at Alnor...

Besides the sight of Bill's bum-crack when he bent over for an attack, it was a beautiful view out of the window. It had rained yesterday, so during the walk to school I had seen sky and clouds in the puddles and smelled that day-after-rain smell.

The air felt great, and on the street, strangers were smiling and saying hi to other strangers. I was feeling good too. This morning I'd woken up before my alarm clock went off. I was wearing my best underwear. All of this gave me the unshakeable feeling that things were going well.

13

"Did you hear me, Hank?" Frankie asked.

"You bet."

My other best friend, Ashley, raised her eyebrows and opened her locker. "So what's your answer?"

"Two weeks," I said. "Two weeks is my answer."

Just then, I saw Karen, the prettiest and most popular girl in school, come around the corner, laughing with a friend. I was feeling so good about things that I gave her my best smile ... and she smiled back!

"Check out that cat," I said, and pointed out of the window.

But the cat wasn't there any more. And I was pointing right at Bill's bum as he swept the puddles off the tarmac.

"Why are you so gross?" Karen's snooty friend, Rachel, said as she clutched her snooty notebook. Both of them grimaced before hurrying away.

"She'll come round," I said.

14

"In two weeks?" Frankie smirked at Ashley.

I was getting the feeling that two weeks was not the correct answer. Two weeks is usually a pretty good answer to almost any question. When is your maths test? *Two weeks*. When will you pay me back that fiver? *Two weeks*. When will you grow up, Henry? *Two weeks!*

"Anyway," Ashley said, "this Saturday Frankie and I are hanging out at Spitalfields shopping centre. You in?"

"Absolutely," I said.

"You sure?" Frankie asked. "It's only two days from now."

"I'll slot you in."

Ashley slammed her locker shut and we headed to class. "Awesome. It was amazing last week, and—"

"—And this week," Frankie said, "they're setting up a movie screen to show *The Slug with Nine Brains*."

"And don't forget: the new limited edition

Tinkodoma Smiley Friend goes on sale at
two o'clock," Ashley said.

"And I bet everyone's going to be there,"
Frankie added.

"Will your parents let you come, Hank?"
Ashley asked.

"Of course."

"They didn't last time," Frankie said.

"Or the time before that," Ashley said.
"Why will this time be different?"

"Two weeks."

Again, not the right answer. Here's
a question that "two weeks" answers
perfectly: how long will it take Hank to
become the biggest loser in Westbrook
Academy?

You see, this Saturday was the second
time that Ashley, Frankie and just about
everyone else in my year had been allowed
to hang out at Spitalfields without adult
supervision. Their parents trusted them
to look after themselves. My parents

barely trusted me to use the microwave. It was so totally unfair. You zapped a magnet in the microwave just the once and you were branded for life with words like "unreliable", "not trustworthy", "immature". Well, starting now, I was no longer a house cat. I was going to be like Alnor the Orange. I was going to fight off the broom of oppression with my razor-sharp claws. I was going to lap up water from the puddle of freedom...

It occurred to me that acting like a stray cat wouldn't exactly calm my parents' nerves.

"Focus, Hank," Frankie said. "Your parents won't let you come, 'cause they think you're not responsible, right?"

"They don't think, they *know*," I said.

"So change their minds," Ashley said. "Prove that you can take care of yourself."

"How?"

"Do something grown-up," Frankie said.

"Like, start shaving?"

17

"Like you have anything to shave, anyway," Ashley said.

As I paused to stroke my chin — where I could feel the beginnings of the luxurious beard that would grow in three years' time — I caught sight of Alnor the Orange again. We were at the end of the corridor now, near the noticeboard and the door to the playground, and I could see through the glass that Alnor was just outside. He'd found a kid's lunchbox and was nuzzling through it. I had to admire the cat's gritty independence. And then I had it! The perfect way to prove to my parents that I was responsible.

"That's what I'll do," I cried and clapped my hands. "I'll cook my family a big dinner all by myself. I'll make beef Wellington and potato gratin, and a spring salad. And for dessert—"

"Stick to something you can handle," Ashley said.

"Like cinnamon toast," said Frankie.

"But I hardly *ever* have accidents any more. I'm as spry as a cat." I flung out my arms, claws extended. But at that very moment, a very strange and mysterious force in the universe was active, because my right arm slammed into a solid block of Antarctic ice.

"Mr Zipzer," a voice hissed like a frigid wind onto the back of my neck. The voice belonged to the one and only Miss Adolf.

"Oh, sorry, Miss. I was just showing my mates here my catlike— I mean, I didn't see you lurking there," I said.

"Burglars and tabloid reporters *lurk*, Henry. I was simply checking this." She pointed at the noticeboard.

"You want to buy Haley Manning's pet turtle?" I asked.

"What on earth would *I* want with a turtle?"

"Right there," I said. "Haley Manning is

19

selling her pet turtle for five quid and—"
I stopped talking because Ashley suddenly
cried out. Her rucksack had slipped from her
hands, and all the blood was draining from
her face, like she'd lost her life force.

"Survival Camp," Ashley gasped as
she looked at where Miss Adolf had been
pointing.

"Correct," Miss Adolf said with a firm
nod. "I was checking the sign-up sheet,
Henry. Would you children care to enlist?
Only two days left to sign up."

Ashley stood, paralyzed, while Frankie,
who was all hunched over, tried to hide
behind her. "Um, uh, we would," he said
into her jumper, "but we can't, because ...
because—"

"Frankie has lice," I said. "In fact, we've
all got them." I started scratching and
slapping myself all over. Frankie and Ashley
followed suit a nanosecond later. "The
itching is not too bad, but we'd hate to

spread our terrible affliction."

A low, guttural sound came from Miss Adolf. It was almost like the sound you hear at the dentist when they're sucking out your saliva with that suction tube. But grosser. She put her hands in her hair and backed away, wide-eyed.

"It's this rare breed of Amazonian jumping lice," I said, scratching my head in obvious torment. "You should see how far they can jump. Or maybe you shouldn't. Save yourself, Miss. They're eating us alive!"

Miss Adolf took three little packets from her skirt pocket and laid them on the floor. "Put those on at once and keep them on. And when you get home tonight, apply some anti-lice shampoo!" Then she turned around and broke into a trot. "Filthy, filthy children, just filthy," she muttered.

"That was too close," Frankie said, once she'd turned the corner.

Ashley ripped open one of the packets. "Shower caps. She keeps spare *shower caps* in her skirt pockets."

"What's really weird," Frankie said, "is that she has *any* names on her list for Survival Camp. Who'd be mad enough to sign up for a weekend of torture?"

Here's what you need to know about Miss Adolf's Survival Camps: they are legendary. And not the good kind of legendary, either, like Cyclops and magical hammers. Miss Adolf's camps are so tough that no one's *ever* made it through the whole weekend. Most kids need years of therapy after. There was this one kid, Allan Kelley, who went three years ago, and he still hasn't recovered. He just sort of sits in his room now, looking at his fish tank and laughing softly. Personally, I'd gladly wear a shower cap until the summer holidays rather than *enlist*. What lunatic would add their name to that list?

"Move, Zitzer," said a voice.

It was my mortal nemesis. Nick McKelty. And he was headed straight for the noticeboard.

"Watch closely, Zitzer," he said. "This is how you write your name. Practise hard and you'll learn to do it too ... when you're twenty."

"I'll be living in a rigid airship when I'm twenty, and you'll still be living on stupid solid ground and writing your name in stupid places." I tapped the back of his pencil, so he drew a wild squiggly line all over the sign-up sheet. "Have fun at Camp Carnage."

"Being a man is about more than fun," McKelty said. "You'd know that if—"

"OK, boys," Ashley said, leading Frankie and me away. "Let's hit the showers." She handed out the caps.

We put them on as we headed to class. We got a few odd looks, but at least we weren't crazy enough to sign up to Miss Adolf's camp. Unlike McKelty.

23

But somewhere between watching Alnor and Bill fight in the playground and arriving at class, I'd lost the good feeling I'd woken up with. Now I had this sinking feeling that I'd be writing my name on that sign-up sheet. Something in me was waking up. Something that sought the wild. Something that wanted to test its strength against all that is unholy!

Then I remembered something crucial. I may have a funky brain, but I'm not mad. Well, maybe I'm a tiny bit mad sometimes. But I will never, *ever* be mad enough to go to Miss Adolf's Camp Carnage.

CHAPTER THREE

"Hey, champ," my dad said as I walked into our flat that afternoon. He was packing up his laptop bag. "Heading out in five to cover a bridge tournament." In case you didn't know, Dad's a sports reporter. He covers all manner of weird and wonderful sports, even sports that aren't even sports, like card games. "You'll be OK on your own till Mum and Emily get in from the deli?"

"No problem," I said and collapsed on the sofa.

"Good. See you for dinner." He reached

over to ruffle my hair. "Should I ask about the shower cap?"

"It's my chef's hat. I'm cooking dinner for everyone tonight."

"Really? Well, just stay away from the micro—"

"I know," I grunted.

"Cooking dinner shows initiative, son. I like it. I'll text the girls and tell them to get ready for a feast."

Then he left, and I had the entire wonderful flat all to my wonderful self. I stretched out and breathed easy.

School had gone by in a blink. No one had really bothered us about the shower caps. The one and only time somebody tried — this kid named Maurice — I lifted up my shower cap and scratched my head really hard in his general direction. From the look on his face, I'm guessing Maurice probably went straight from school to the barber for a buzz cut. Personally, I think

Miss Adolf figured out we didn't *really* have Amazonian jumping lice when Ashley took off her shower cap. Eventually Frankie did too. But not me.

It had been my plan all along to start work on my dinner feast first thing after school. I had to prove to my parents once and for all that I could look after myself – and what better way than by cooking a meal for the whole family?

But before I could get busy in the kitchen, I had to look up some recipes online, and I obviously couldn't go on the Internet without watching that screaming goat on YouTube. I really liked that screaming goat. I had probably watched that screaming goat about twelve times.

Then I threw all the sofa cushions on the floor for no real reason and kind of forgot about my plan. For an hour or two I just sort of rolled around on the floor and practised making goatish noises. Then I started to wonder how Emily's iguana, Katherine, would react to my goatish noises, so I went to find her. She was hibernating or something in Emily's wardrobe.

It was really hot in Emily's room, and all the lights were out. Emily had left a little stereo that played jungle sound effects in the wardrobe. No matter how loudly I screamed, Katherine wouldn't budge from her spot on top of Emily's laundry basket.

I'm not really sure what I did after that. I either played mind-piercing notes on Emily's flute to Katherine or I looked through Emily's drawers. Either way, by the time I remembered to start on the feast, it was getting dark outside.

There wasn't enough time to look up a recipe, so I had to wing it, Zipzer style. I put on Mum's apron, tightened my shower cap, and scoured the kitchen for edible foodstuffs. The pickings were slim. We had some chicken breasts, but they leaked out this gross fluid, and it turns out that touching raw chicken gives me the ickiest feeling.

Other than the icky chicken, the rest of the meat department was very poorly stocked. There was a whole greenish-coloured fish that my grandpa Papa Pete must have fished out of the gutter last month. It was pretty slimy *and* it was looking at me. (Papa Pete doesn't live with us, but he is always leaving things in our freezer.) We also had one old sausage that was pretty much the same colour as the fish.

I did find a huge bag of rice in the cupboard, so I thought I'd start there. Get the rice going, you know, and build around it. It was hard to read the directions on the rice packet, because the writing was really small and my brain doesn't like really small writing, but also because I'd sliced a hole in the bag right where the instructions were.

I knew I needed water and a saucepan. And then I heard a tinkling sound and realized I'd been leaving a trail of rice across the kitchen.

"You're too complicated, rice," I said and hurled the packet down.

I had almost identical problems with a box of couscous, a box of bow-tie pasta and a bag of lentils.

The fridge was, of course, overflowing with fresh veggies — carrots, aubergines, spinach, some sort of yellowish type thing — but washing and peeling and cutting up all those veggies seemed like a huge chore. Far too big a chore just to eat some veggies.

If you want to know the truth, I was starting to feel pretty down in the dumps. Everything was either gross or too complicated. I was about ready to hang up my chef's cap (shower cap) and go and watch the snoring gorilla video when I had a thought so horrible that I slumped to the floor. *What if I never learned to take care of myself?*

I imagined being, like, twenty or something really old, with a moustache, of course, and walking hand-in-hand with my parents around Spitalfields shopping centre. Then, while my dad was tying my shoelace and my mum was wiping my nose, McKelty wafted by in *his* rigid airship and chucked a tomato at my head.

I would never let that happen.

Come on, Zipper Man, buck up. You're wearing the hat, so be the chef. Don't dishonour the chef's profession. Give yourself a manly slap to the cheek and get cooking!

I scanned the kitchen again, this time with fresh eyes. *Now, keep it simple,* I told myself, *just like Ashley said.* One thing we had plenty of was pickles. We always do. Because pickles are probably the perfect food. And they go with every meal. I popped the lid off a jar of beautiful kosher dill pickles and poured them in a bowl. Veggies: check!

Then I looked around for other simple and delicious dinner ideas. We had three cans of baked beans and a whole loaf of sliced bread... *Beans on toast! What could be easier? The recipe was in the name.*

I switched on the radio to the Latin jazz station, which is what Dad always listens to when he's cooking, got the toast in the toaster, the beans in a pot, and lit the flame while I shimmied and rhumba-ed around the kitchen.

I knew I wasn't cooking up a gourmet dinner, but everyone knows dinner is just an appetizer for ... dessert. And the only proper dessert is, of course, chocolate cake. I had that covered. I'd watched Mum make that a million times.

I got out the flour and poured it into a mixing bowl before sliding over to the stove and stirring the beans. Then I tapped my way back to the mixing bowl and poured in the sugar. Then a little more sugar. And then all the sugar fell out of the box in one clump onto the worktop. *Egad!*

The beans were bubbling, so there was no time to clean up properly. I had to improvise. I lowered my mouth to worktop level and shovelled most of the sugar right in. Then I tapped back to the beans before soft-shoeing over to the toaster.

I turned up the tunes all the way. I was starting to feel pretty good. Cooking was a snap. This was going to work! I got the eggs out of the fridge, cracked one into the mixing bowl, tossed the shells over my shoulder, and soon I was singing.

The front door slammed. It was Mum and Emily. They were bickering like mad.

"I'm not being mean. I just don't think you're ready," Mum said.

"But, Mum, what you fail to understand is that—"

"Is something burning? Hank, is that you? *Haaannk!*"

Hearing my mum's voice made me see the entire kitchen through "mum" eyes. All our food was out and opened. Much of it was on the floor, snaking around the kitchen in little trails. Smoke was billowing from the hob and the toaster. It was getting hard to breathe, and hot!

My beans! My toast! They were ruined!

And the cake mix looked like, well, you don't *really* want to know what it looked like.

I had approximately 1.4 seconds before Mum got here, which was not enough time to perfect my feast, or hide the evidence. So I shovelled the rest of the sugar into my mouth and hurled the cake bowl, still full of mixture, into the cupboard.

"Oh, Hank. What have you done?" Mum cried.

"Hi, Mama! You hungry?"

She didn't answer. She was too busy dashing around the kitchen, opening windows, fanning smoke, stepping on eggshells and sighing aggressively.

And from across the flat came another voice. "Why were you in my *room*?" Emily yelled.

I took off my chef's cap, tossed it into the sink and flipped on the waste disposal.

"Oh, Hank, for the love of..." cried my mum.

CHAPTER FOUR

"It is a pretty good dinner, Hank," Papa Pete said. "The pickles are very tasty."

"Thanks, Papa Pete!" I said.

He smiled and took another bite of the pickle. "Mmm." Then it was back to the dreadful silence of people eating burned toast and beans and breathing angrily.

Mum took a bite of black toast. She choked it down with a gagging sound while glaring at me. Emily dragged her fork through charred beans and glared at Mum. Dad spent an eternity scraping the charred parts off his toast. When he finally took a bite, he erupted into a full-on coughing fit until the veins started popping out in his forehead.

"Drink," Papa Pete said, handing him a glass of water.

Dad drank and stared at me, clearing his throat every few seconds to remind me that my food had almost literally killed him. No one apart from Papa Pete had talked the whole meal.

Papa Pete took another huge chomp of the pickle, drank a huge gulp of water and said, "Ahhh. The water is very good, too, Hank."

Mum threw her fork down and sighed. "Don't humour him. This dinner—"

"—This dinner," Dad interrupted, clearing his throat again, "perfectly illustrates why you aren't ready to go to Spitalfields on your own, Hank."

I opened my mouth to say that I wouldn't

be cooking beans at Spitalfields, but Papa Pete spoke up for me.

"It was his first time. A good try. Let him practise. Gain experience. Rome wasn't built in a day, you know."

"But he almost burned it down in an evening," my mum said.

"Rome?" Papa Pete asked.

"Yes," she said. "This flat is my Rome. I am the empress of this flat, and in one evening, he destroyed all my food and nearly burned down my empire, not to mention what he did to my waste disposal."

"*Your* waste disposal?" My dad waved a hand that was wrapped in bloody bandages. "After I sacrificed my good hand fixing it, I would say that it was *my*—"

Emily set her glass down with a thud and snorted.

"Oh, what now?" my dad said.

"For once, can the dinnertime conversation be about something *other* than

Hank's mental problems?"

"Of course, sweetie," Dad said. "It's not like anyone ever wants to talk about my mental—"

"Or the amount of smoke I inhaled," Mum said.

"Or the horrible injury to my hand," Dad said. "But go ahead, Emily. What do *you* want to talk about?"

"Three items, thank you." She took a piece of paper from her lap, unfolded it carefully and laid it flat on the table next to her notebook. "One, why did Mum throw away this take-your-child-to-work letter?" She peeled a slice of tomato off the sheet of paper and chucked it at my ear.

"Er..." My mum took a very long sip of water. "I told you that was a mix-up, sweetie. The letter must have fallen out—"

Emily ignored her. "Two, why won't Mum help me to complete my take-your-child-to-work assignment by letting me spend a day with her at the deli?" She opened her notebook to a very complicated-looking graph. "Aside from it being a *compulsory* piece of homework, I believe I can help you. I've noticed a number of inefficiencies that I could streamline. Look." She tapped the graph.

"I'd like to hear your ideas," Papa Pete said.

"No!" Mum said quickly. "Emily, you coming to work with me ... just isn't a good idea. Remember when Dad took Hank to cover the Olympics and Hank sunbathed on the beach volleyball court? Not to mention the sandcastle—"

"Three, why do I have to suffer every time Hank does something stupid?" Emily prodded the pile of baked beans with her fork like she was dissecting a frog.

Dad picked up a charcoaled crust of toast with his injured hand, gasping to show that he was in great pain. After gagging the toast down, he said, "Everyone is suffering tonight, Em."

"But no one has answered any of my questions."

"Stan, Rosa, can I say something?" Papa Pete asked, and then went on even though no one had said he could. "The kids need to learn about life *from* life. See the real world and how it works. When I was a boy, I could make a wild boar into salami with my bare hands. They want this too. Maybe not the wild boar, but you know what I mean, eh?"

"No," my dad said, trying to grip his fork in his bad hand. "What do you mean?"

"You are both too ... over-protective."

My mum's nostrils were seriously flaring. "Over-protective?!"

"Maybe that's too strong a word."

"No more words from anyone," Mum said. "Your empress has spoken." She sliced her knife through the charred toast, cutting it for what seemed like five minutes. When she

41

finally put a slice in her mouth and chewed, it sounded like exploding fire crackers.

Dad went on eating with his bad hand and looking worriedly at the bandages, while Emily sat with her arms folded, flaring her nostrils just like Mum. Papa Pete kept looking around at everyone, trying to catch someone's eye to soften the awkwardness.

It was unbearable. I just lowered my head and tried to pretend that my beans were edible. They were not. They were unedible. They weren't even beans any more. They were unbeanable. But I would have eaten everyone's beans and had seconds if it meant that I didn't have to sit at that table a second longer.

Somewhere, on a balcony in the distance, a dog was howling into the night. I kind of wanted to be out there with that dog. Not with *that* dog. Or on a balcony. But I kind of wanted to be out in the wild with *wild* dogs. Normally, living with my brain is like clicking

42

through all the TV channels, rapid fire. But for a few moments while I listened to that dog, a single channel was coming through, clear and direct.

I knew why my cooking-for-freedom plan had failed. I had tried to prove to my parents that I was capable. And that was the problem. What I needed to do was prove it to myself. I also had a pretty good idea of how to do that. But that idea was more horrific than my baked beans. It was so horrific that I took a huge bite of beans just to flush it from my brain.

Papa Pete took another swig from his glass and said, "It really is very good water, Hank."

CHAPTER FIVE

"You don't look good," Ashley said to me
the next morning as she and Frankie met me
at my front door.

"I don't feel good, either."

We got in the lift.

"You're all greasy," she said, "and paler
than normal, and your eyes ... are all
bloodshot."

"I had a sugar vision last night."

"A what?" Ashley felt my forehead and
checked my pulse. "I think you need a doctor.
Let's go back and I'll get my medic's kit."

"I'm fine, Ash," I said. "I just ate, like, a kilo of sugar, so I was kicking and squirming all night. Plus, I was having all these weird dreams about giant slugs because I ate a load of charred baked beans."

"Baked beans? You put sugar in baked beans? What happened to the cinnamon toast?" Frankie asked.

"It's complicated, Frankie," I said. "Let's just say the cooking-for-freedom plan was a complete disaster. But late last night, I had a moment of – whaddyacallit? – clarity. I know what I have to do. I heard the wolf's call, and I must answer it, even though I don't want to. A part of me has already answered it. The wild, you see, I must go yonder into the—"

"He's talking gibberish," Ashley said to Frankie as we got out of the lift. "Get him to lie down here while I get my kit."

"Nah, he's all right," Frankie said. "Now, I'm talking to Regular Hank. Nod your head if you can hear me, Regular Hank?"

I nodded.

"Regular Hank, are you coming with us to Spitalfields tomorrow or not?"

"Not tomorrow, my oldest and truest friends. But if I live, and I will, I'll be there in two weeks."

They tried to talk me out of it the whole walk to school. I also tried to talk myself out of it, which made Ashley uncomfortable. She was worried I was feverish and kept asking me if I needed to stop and have a rest. But I didn't stop walking until we were standing in front of the school noticeboard.

"There's got to be another way," Ashley said.

"Think about it," I said. "If I can survive a weekend in the wild with Miss Adolf, my parents will see that I can survive an afternoon at the shopping centre."

"What good is a shopping centre if you're

a corpse?" Frankie said as I wrote my name on the list. "You'll never make it, mate. Or you'll be horribly injured. Or dead *and* horribly injured."

"You think there'll be horrible injuries?" Ashley asked.

"It's Miss Adolf's Survival Camp. There are *always* horrible injuries. Remember Ryan Springflower's neck-brace last year?"

"*Oh,* I do. I do remember that." Ashley seemed to be glowing. She grabbed the pencil out of my hand and wrote her name below mine on the sign-up sheet. "Now it's your turn, Frankie."

"Are you kidding? You're both sick. You said it yourself, Ash. Hank is sick. And now you're sick. You've got that disease where the doctor thinks he's got the patient's disease. What's that disease called?"

"Don't change the subject," I said to him. "Come on — you can't let us go without you."

47

"Watch me."

"Come on, old buddy, old pal. You want to go."

"Um, no."

"You want to go. You must go. You feel your arm moving—"

"Stop using the Force on me. It won't work."

"But it's working already. See for yourself."

And his arm really was moving!

"You want to write your name," I said.

"I don't."

"You *will* write your name. You will write your name and then you will join us."

"Never!"

"Join us!"

"This is the Dark Side," Frankie said. He was writing his name while practically in tears. "You've changed, Hank! You've changed!"

Just then the school bell rang, and it

sounded so loud and shrill that we all took off in a sprint for class, hearts racing. But it also broke the spell, and I cried out, "What have we done?"

CHAPTER SIX

My mum asked pretty much the same thing when she found the permission slip in my bag and realized what it was for. She's always looking through my bag without asking ... and always finding disciplinary letters in there. Mostly because I don't show her the disciplinary letters. So, I don't really blame her for looking through my bag without asking.

"I can't believe you're doing this. Are you mad?" she said, clearly in shock.

"It'll prove I can look after myself."

"There are kids still in therapy from last year's trip. And what about that boy, that boy who just looks at his fish tank all day?"

"Allan Kelley? Oh, that's a legend."

"Right here." She pointed to a line of the slip. "It says in bold letters, 'All pupils will be injured in some capacity.' That's not a legend. That's a binding contract. I'm not signing it."

"Ah, let him go," Papa Pete said from the kitchen. He was cooking tonight, and thank goodness for that. With his cooking knife, he sliced a tomato into a million pieces in two seconds. "When I was his age, I—"

"When you were his age, it was a different world."

"Yes, it was," Papa Pete said. "If you wanted to be somebody, you had to prove yourself. You had to go outside and build a fire. My father taught me how to be a man!"

My mum looked over at my dad, who was

sitting at the table, hunched over his laptop. "Care to join us, Stan?"

He was mumbling words into his screen. "'... But I don't mean to trouble you, of course. So if you have a moment, could you kindly forward me the 'Hubolt' file, but only if you have it handy. Please don't bother if it isn't handy. It's not very important at all, and I'm sure I can manage without it. In fact, forget I even mentioned it. Just pretend you never got this email. Kindest regards, Stan.' Aaaa—nd send."

"Stan!"

"Oh, right. I give him plenty of lessons on how to be a man, right, Hank?"

"What do you teach him?" Papa Pete asked. He was now pounding out some dough. "How to write a friendly email? How to use a Satnav?" He pointed the knife at Dad. "That is not a man."

Dad bristled. "Last week I showed him

how to unclog the printer. And the week before that I showed him how to sort the recycling..." Dad closed his laptop with a sheepish grin. "Right, yes, OK. Maybe he should go to camp. It'll help him learn about, you know, *man* things..."

Mum crossed her arms. "You men and your 'man things'."

"Yes, man things, like nature and self-reliance," Dad said.

"And if I get through camp," I asked, "will you let me go to Spitalfields next weekend?"

"Deal," said Dad.

"Wait! What? I haven't agreed to anything," Mum said.

"And Mum will stop looking through my bag without asking?" I looked at Dad. I was on a roll.

"If he can go to camp," Emily interrupted, emerging from the shadows, "then I should be allowed to work in the deli..."

"I haven't said Hank can go. And, no, I'm sorry, sweetie, but you're just not ready to work at the deli. Don't feel bad about it, 'kay?" Mum said.

"I don't feel bad about it." Emily opened her notebook. She wrote something down and underlined it. "But I will remember it."

"I don't like you keeping notes like that."

"She can go, too," my dad said to my mum, who flared her nostrils at him. Dad, however, turned to Papa Pete. "See? I teach them to be men... Why are looking at me like that, Em? I know you're a girl. I didn't mean *you*, of course. Stop looking at me that way. Emily, please stop looking at me that way. I'm the one letting you go, so look at your mum, OK? She's the one who threw away the letter."

Emily turned to Mum. "Can I bring my lizard?"

"This is your fault," Mum said to Dad.

Dad quickly opened his laptop so his face was hidden by the screen.

"Don't look at me," he mumbled. "Look at Hank."

CHAPTER SEVEN

People often tell me I'm an underachiever, but no one has ever said to me, "Hank, you're over-thinking it," which I take as a compliment. The way I see it, most things don't really require that much thinking. Most real-world things turn out OK whether you think really hard about them or not.

Take packing a bag. Everyone I know thinks it's really complicated and time-consuming. Whenever we go on holiday, my parents start bugging me to pack my bag, like, a decade in advance. Seriously, it's as if my dad thinks I should be spending an hour every night just packing a bag or thinking about what I'm going to pack in a bag. But what's to think about? You just throw a toothbrush and whatever cleanish clothes you can find into a bag and zip it up. Ten minutes, tops. Maybe I'm just really good at zipping?

And if you forget your socks or something, you can always buy extra, or "borrow" some from Emily.

But this time I did a lot of thinking about what to pack. Too much thinking. Because when you get down to it, packing a bag is like predicting the future. Some futures are easy to predict. Like when we went to the beach last summer, I packed a towel, my flip-flops and my Spiderman Speedos. Just kidding about the Speedos...

... Or am I?

Miss Adolf's Survival Camp, on the other hand, was totally unpredictable. I knew we'd be at a campsite for two days, and that was all I knew. The location of the site wasn't even listed on the permission slip. It was "undisclosed". There are lots of legends about the camp, but there's no solid intel. Kids who have gone don't want to talk about it. The memories are too painful.

I could hear my family talking about me in the next room, saying things like, "Hank's not up to the challenge," and "I bet he forgets to pack socks, and the one pair he has gets wet." Then Emily said that if your feet are wet for too long you get trench foot, and the only cure for trench foot is amputation.

So with my survival (and my feet) on the line, I had to take this packing job very seriously. The last thing I wanted was to flunk Survival Camp because I'd forgotten to pack something I couldn't survive without. But other than plenty of socks (thanks, Emily), what kind of stuff do you need to survive?

*First things first, Zipper Man, you need
a rucksack to hold all of your awesome
survival gear.*

My bag was in the bottom corner of my
wardrobe, and before I found it, I had to
throw nearly everything I owned into a pile
in the middle of my room. That took forever,
and I very deliberately made a ton of extra
noise. So while my family went on discussing
how tough it would be to care for a double
amputee, at least it would sound like I was
doing some serious packing.

I threw every clean pair of socks I owned
into my rucksack. Next up: trousers. But
what kind of trousers, and how many? That
was when I really started to over-think.

They always say to pack light in survival
situations. But if I packed too light and
didn't take enough trousers, I might have to
wear wet and muddy ones, and then I'd get
hypothermia and fail the camp.

But if I packed too many trousers, my

pack would weigh a ton, and Miss Adolf might make us carry our packs everywhere, or make us run up a mountain with them on our backs, and since mine would be the heaviest, I'd fall behind, and everyone knows that predators attack the stragglers.

The problem was the unpredictability. Then I realized something. This was *Miss Adolf's* camp. So I had to think like Miss Adolf. Enter her world. What would she think I'd need to survive?

None of my stuff looked even remotely "survivally". I kept expecting to find awesome survival stuff in my wardrobe, like hatchets, bear-traps and night-vision goggles, but all I found was a bunch of my old, broken toys. I started to feel pretty sorry for myself. After a while I just sat down on my bed, holding my nearly empty rucksack on my lap until there was a knock on the door.

"You can't come in," I said and dived onto

the ground to start rummaging through my junky belongings. "I'm packing!"

My dad and Papa Pete came in anyway.

"Looks like a thorough packing job, champ," Dad said. "Not bad."

Not bad was probably the best compliment Dad had given me in nine months, so I played it cool. "You know me," I said as I contemplated my old lightsabre with a serious look and then threw it in the rucksack.

"I'm proud of you for signing up," he continued. "And I've got something special for you." He patted his trouser pockets. "Where did I...?"

None of his pockets were bulging, so it had to be a very small, special something. Then I realized that this was the moment I'd been waiting for my whole life. Dad was going to give me a penknife!

"I have something for you, too," Papa Pete said.

He sat on my bed and took out this small silver box. It was sort of rusty and textured and old-looking, but in an awesome way, like it had magical powers. On the lid was a faded engraving of a lion.

I sat on the bed next to him. "What is it?"

"It is a tinderbox. A fire-starting kit. It was my grandfather's. It saved his life when he was shipwrecked after the war. He gave it to me, and now I'm giving it to you."

It felt amazing in my hands. I could feel its history. "Whoa."

"Promise you won't lose it. You must give it to your grandson one day."

"I promise, Papa Pete. Wow, thanks so much."

"It gives me great pride and joy to give it to you. Now, let's see what your dad has brought you."

My dad was just standing there, looking even more uncertain.

"Dad?"

"Right." He got my special something out of his back pocket. My special something was a zip-up plastic bag. "You can put your phone in it. Stop it from getting wet..."

"Oh."

"It zips shut. Easy to use. It's a triumph of modern technology, if you think about it."

"Um, thanks?"

"You bet, champ." He patted my shoulder awkwardly. "Now, I better get to that recycling."

A penknife would have been pretty sweet, of course, and a major father-son bonding moment, but his gift made me realize how much my dad and I have in common. I, too, buy my presents from the bottom drawer. At least my bottom drawer has one-of-a-kind items, though, like the chewing-gum-and-pen-cap sculpture it had made after years of mysterious activity. I gave that to Emily for her birthday.

But the zip-up bag was good too. And it gave me an idea. What I needed was more bags. For food! Food was the ultimate survival gear. Food to eat. Food to trade for favours and protection – because there was no guarantee Miss Adolf would feed us at all.

In the kitchen, Mum and Emily were doing some mother-daughter bonding. Mum had given Emily a pair of bright-yellow rubber gloves. I didn't want to spoil the moment, so I did my best Emily impersonation and lurked in the shadows.

"… because tomorrow at the deli," Mum said, "you'll be doing the washing-up."

"Are you trying to keep me out of the way?" Emily asked.

"Of course not. Now, put this in that cupboard." She gave Emily a clean mixing bowl.

Emily sighed. "Are you scared my

superior business abilities will expose you as a failure?" She opened the cupboard under the sink and found the mixing bowl I'd hidden in there yesterday. She sniffed it. "Ew, what is—?"

"Tonobungay!" I shouted, materializing out of the ether to snatch the mixing bowl from Emily's yellow, rubber paws. "Mine! Special camping food." After grabbing a Tupperware tub, I poured the sand-coloured slop into it.

Emily watched me the whole time. "That's not camping food."

"Of course it is."

"Of course it *isn't*."

"Don't argue with the customer. Mum, in the restaurant business, isn't the customer always right?"

"Hank, are you packed?" Mum asked.

"Uh-huh."

"We're getting an early start, so you better be."

"You're not the customer," Emily interrupted. "And that's not camping food."

"You're wearing yellow gloves, Em, and I'm holding food. That makes me the customer and you the lowly employee."

"That's not even food. Doesn't smell like food."

"It tastes like food." I pretended to eat some and rubbed my belly. "Mmm."

"You're not eating it."

"Am too."

"Give me that Tupperware." And she lunged for it.

"Mum, your employee is harassing me!"

"Emily," my mum said, exasperated, "the customer is always right. Dry those dishes. At once, young lady. I'm the empress."

I made for another drawer, grabbed a stack of plastic bags and started loading them up with biscuits.

"What are you doing?" Mum confiscated my biscuit bags and chucked them, along

66

with all the remaining biscuits and sweets, into a ten-centimetre space between the top of the kitchen cabinets and the ceiling. "Go and pack. And back to work, Emily. Chop-chop."

As I walked back to my room, I heard Emily say to Mum, "If you try to keep me down, I will rise up against you."

CHAPTER EIGHT

I woke up the next morning, and started screaming, because it was the next morning. It was today, and today was the beginning of the end. Today I would die at Survival Camp!

There was a knock on my door.

"Everything all right in there?" Mum asked.

"Just a bad dream, Mum. I'm fine."

"Good. We're leaving in ten. Are you ready?"

The nightmare was ongoing. I couldn't wake up from it. I had slept through my alarm clock. And on the floor was my rucksack, and apart from plenty of socks, Papa Pete's tinderbox, Dad's zip-up plastic bag and a Tubberware container of cake mix, it was totally unpacked. I screamed again!

"You're going to *fail*," hissed a voice.

I looked up to see that Emily had cracked the door open and was looking in at me with the evil eye. Katherine's evil eye was also looking at me.

"Get out, vile woman!"

"Beware the lizard's curse!" She chuckled as she closed the door.

I threw my head back onto the pillow, and gave myself two minutes. Two minutes just to rest my eyes. Two minutes just for myself. Just two minuuuuteeeesssss...

BANG BANG BANG!

"Are you up?" It was my mum again. "We're leaving in five minutes!"

CHAPTER NINE

"You're going to be so late, Hank." My mum
was driving fast, really fast. I was slumped
all the way down in the front seat, covering
my eyes and moaning aloud while making a
smacking sound with my lips.

"Stop moaning," Mum said.

"I can't."

"Hank, it was your mad idea to go to this
camp." Mum gunned the engine, then made
a sharp right turn that threw me against the
door. "And I can't believe you waited till this
morning to pack. You're going to be so late."

"Don't worry. The coach doesn't leave till nine."

"I don't know what you packed in that bag of yours, but it smells rotten."

"Can't you go faster, Mum? It's six minutes to nine."

"Good. You have six minutes to change your mind about going." Mum came to a screeching stop to avoid rear-ending a lorry and blasted her horn. "What are you doing?" she shouted at the driver.

Maybe it was the brush with death, or maybe it was the fumes from my bag, or maybe it was both — but at that moment, it felt as though I might only have six minutes left to live.

And I wanted to live!

But I also wanted to go to Spitalfields. And that meant proving I was responsible by surviving Camp Carnage. There was no backing out now. Unless...

I groaned and — I'm not proud of this —

I put my whole head in my T-shirt to try and knock myself out by breathing in the CO_2 in my shirt.

Three lousy minutes later, I was still breathing, and the car came to a stop.

"What is this?" my mum asked.

"What?"

She yanked my T-shirt down.

"Looks like an empty car park," I said.

"Good, Hank. And what do you *not* see?"

"The coach."

"What time did you say it left?"

"Nine. Or eight, maybe. Or some other number, like tomorrow."

"Hank, you don't have to go to camp."

"I know."

"I can just take you home. Or we can go for a pancake breakfast. Just the two of us."

No! I couldn't do that. Frankie and Ashley were waiting for me at Camp Carnage. I couldn't let them down. And a week into the future, a super-cool kid named Hank "the

Zipper Man" Zipzer was waiting for me at Spitalfields. *I couldn't let the Zipper Man down either.*

"Mum, drive me to Survival Camp. Please."

She frowned at me as she pulled out of the car park and back onto the road. And as for the Zipper Man, I slumped all the way down in my seat. Then I covered my eyes and made a smacking sound with my lips again.

"Stop moaning," Mum said.

"I can't!" I wailed.

CHAPTER TEN

**From the pages of Emily Zipzer's field
notebook...**

11:30 a.m., 7th May

I arrived at the deli at 08:59, precisely. First
impressions: the deli is run inefficiently.
They do not keep electronic records,
and this leaves both deli and customers
operating at a loss.

Example: this morning Papa Pete baked
forty-five cranberry muffins and only

eight blueberry muffins. An hour after opening, they had sold out of blueberry muffins and had not sold a single cranberry muffin. I mentioned to Papa Pete that if he kept better records, he could establish a predictive model, but he did not hear me out. He said he runs the deli with his "feelings".

The mother soon arrived. She was late. Hank had, of course, missed his coach, and she had to drive him to camp. He will be tardy to his Survival Camp. Miss Adolf will mark him down for his tardiness.

I hope the lizard's curse contributed to this. (As a natural scientist, I do not believe in magic, but Hank does. I know he'll be worrying about the curse. I do regret exploiting Katherine for my vengeance. Perhaps I will let her sleep in bed with me tonight.)

When the mother arrived at the deli, she gave Papa Pete a list of things he should not allow me to do. Papa Pete told her he did not need such a list, and that she was being over-protective. He said he could handle things here and gave the mother the day off.

Papa Pete is a man of "feelings" and not data. He considers himself my ally. I can exploit his "feelings". I can make him my tool. By hook or by crook, I will control him.

The mother soon noticed me observing and writing these notes. She watches now as I write this. She must wonder if I am writing about her. My notes make her uncomfortable. Clearly, she fears that I will uncover her incompetence. She has made every effort to keep me away from this deli. As a scientist, one must get into the habit of asking why.

Working hypothesis: the mother fears that I am more capable of running the Spicy Salami deli than she and Papa Pete are.

I am in good spirits as I write this, and

hopeful for what the day will bring. Let this field notebook be a record of my deeds.

Today I plant the first seeds of my empire!

CHAPTER ELEVEN

"Bye, Mum!" I called out as her car screeched away. I didn't get much of a goodbye. Or any goodbye. Just sort of a look that said if she opened her mouth, I wouldn't like what came out of it. I don't know why she was mad. She knows I'm no good at reading a map. What are those microscopic, squiggly lines for anyway? A map should look like what you'll see on the road as you drive.

Here's what should have been on the map:

A bridge.

A brownish tree.

A barn.

Some sheep.

Another barn.

A cow that looked at me.

The inside of my shirt and a fraction of my left nipple.

A waterslide park.

A camel, a llama and an alpaca.

A barn with cows sitting down outside it.

A golf course.

A pond.

And we're here.

Here was just an empty, muddy field. A minibus was parked beside it. I had arrived super late. All the kids were on the other side of the field. Most of them were lying on the ground. The few kids still standing were hoisting their packs up and down in the air. Miss Adolf, in a full safari khaki short-suit with knee socks and wide-brimmed hat, was blowing a whistle at them.

"Hank!" someone shouted. It was Ashley coming towards me. "You've missed loads of injuries." She was supporting Jonah Gottlieb, who was covered in mud from head to toe and looking off to a faraway place.

"Good ones?"

"Oh, yeah." She slapped Jonah lightly a few times to rouse him. He was unresponsive. "I brought my smelling salts," she said, placing a little packet under his nostrils.

Jonah snapped to and immediately started coughing up ... mud.

"Miss Adolf's making you eat *mud*?"

"I wish!" Jonah said, his eyes lighting up. He started laughing, then he started sobbing, then he was doing both at the same time.

"You're all right, Jonah," Ashley said. "You're going home."

"She scrambled his brains!" I said.

"Poison ivy on the right arm, stinging nettles on the neck, a twisted ankle, and general mental exhaustion," Ashley said. "Adolf's running a minibus service. They're calling it the Quitters' Express." She pointed at the bus parked on the side of the road. Bill the caretaker was in the driver's seat. Alnor, the orange cat from the playground, was sitting on his shoulders. I waved at both of them but got no response.

Ashley started to walk over to it. "And watch that rucksack," she called back. "Adolf's confiscating anything suspect."

Papa Pete's tinderbox!

"Wait, Ash! Take this back for me." I undid my rucksack and quickly tipped everything out onto the muddy field. My tub of cake mix. My three lightsabres. My plastic Wolverine-claw glove. My mobile phone. My Bermuda shorts. The complimentary T-shirt my weirdo dentist gives away with every

cavity filling. My ten pairs of clean socks ...
hello, trench foot! And the tinderbox.

"Can you take this back to my parents?"
I asked, handing it to Ashley. "It's valuable.
I'll text them to say that you'll bring it by."

"Don't let Adolf see your phone. She
sent them all back on the last minibus."

A whistle pierced the air. It was followed
by a shout of "Henry Zipzer!"

Miss Adolf was heading right for us.
Somehow she seemed to be covering the
ground at the speed of an Olympic sprinter.
As she neared I saw that her nose was
coated in white sunscreen. When Jonah
Gottlieb saw her, he fell to the ground and
started fish flopping.

I quickly shoved my phone down my
trousers.

"See ya," Ashley said quickly, and she
walked off with Jonah the fish to the sad
little bus.

"Ah, Henry Zipzer," Miss Adolf said.

"Only an hour and a half late. If this were a real survival scenario, we'd be eating your corpse by now."

My jaw dropped. "Miss?"

"Yes, Henry, the quick and the dead. And as is always the case, all you can do quickly is make a mess. Let's take a look at what you've brought, then." At great speed, Miss Adolf unfolded a giant retractable prodding stick like it was some sort of flick knife. At the end of it was a rubber finger. It may not have even been made of rubber. She poked through my shoddy belongings. "Excellent work, Henry. I see you've packed all the survival essentials. Three plastic swords..."

"Lightsabres."

"Rubbish." She flipped them up with her poking stick, then caught them and broke them in two, depositing the pieces in one of her pockets. "A plastic hedging claw." This she crushed under her foot, along with my spirit. "And last but not least, what no outdoorsman should ever forget, cake mix."

"That's for you. Frankie and I were going to bake it for you."

"Very humorous, Mr Zipzer, but as you'll see, humour will not save you in the wild. The 'funny' one is, in my experience, the first one to be eaten alive by bears. And I see nothing here that will aid in your survival.

"No jacket, no sleeping bag, no torch," she went on. "No cooking utensils, no signalling apparatus, no water, no water-purification device. How do you intend to survive without water? You're not planning to ... *ahem* ... recycle? If not, you'll just have to dig a well. There's a water source about three metres below the topsoil. Did you bring a survival shovel?"

I couldn't even answer. It's hard to talk when you feel like your spine is being slowly crushed. Or maybe that was just Miss Adolf's prodding stick. She was patting my pockets with the finger. It could have been a real finger. I saw blood. I'm not kidding.

"Where's your mobile phone?"

"Forgot it, Miss."

"That's the first sensible thing you've done today. Now, pack your bag up properly, and add those two rocks to it. We will need them at the campsite. What are you waiting for? The quick and the dead, Henry."

She used her prodding stick to guide my movements, finding those places on my body — like behind my knee or near my armpit — where just a touch can make you lose balance. I was her marionette. And those rocks weren't just rocks, they were boulders.

After I'd repacked, she had me hoist the whole pack over my head and pump it up and down as I jogged to the campsite. Her prodding stick tickled my calves the whole time.

Once I arrived at the campsite, I collapsed … into the mud.

Everyone was setting up tents. I spotted Frankie among them. He was a shell of a man. He'd lost the twinkle in his eye.

"Where do you want the rocks, Miss?" I asked.

"In your pack. They're your burden for being tardy. Now go and set up your tent."

"Yes, Miss."

I collapsed again when I reached Frankie. He was struggling with the tent.

"Gimme your water," was how he greeted me.

"It's eight feet below my bum."

"Help me build this tent, then."

"Can't we just sleep under the stars?"

"And be eaten alive by wild badgers? Get up."

We struggled with the tent for what felt like hours. It was a gorgeous-looking thing in the picture on the box, but no matter what we did, it never resembled much more than a rubbish bag. Finally we got something assembled where one side of it, at least, was a few feet off the ground.

"That'll work," I said.

"It *might* work, if you hadn't pegged my foot to the ground."

The super-taut pole was threaded through Frankie's shoelaces and then into the mud. And that pole was supporting our whole concoction. I kneeled beside him and clawed the tent peg out. Then I lifted it through the lace with a trembling arm — but there was so much pressure that it twanged out of my hand and went whipping through the air, missing my earlobe by less than an inch. Whatever had been "tent-like" about our tent evaporated in a depressing sigh.

"Hank, this is a nightmare."

"It's OK. We can just sleep *under* the tent. Or hang it up like tarpaulin. Or we can make some clothes out of the material. Like a squirrel suit. Then we'll climb up the trees and glide throughout the night. I'm sorry. I'm just really hungry. Maybe I'll get started on the well. And the latrine."

"Do us both a favour and dig *two separate* holes."

A voice came from behind me. "Well, Henry," said Miss Adolf. The rubber finger prodded our tent. "Since your arrival, your team has made *negative* progress. I bet you boys are hungry, yes?"

We just stared up at her with sad orphan eyes.

She produced a bag of instant rice from her khaki short-suit. "Here's your supper." She chucked the packet over the tent into a patch of stinging nettles. "In the wild, nothing comes easily."

"But how will we cook it, Miss?" Frankie asked. "You took my matches."

"See that ridge in the distance?" she asked, and pointed to a featureless spot on the horizon. "Run to it. You may find some flint there. And if not, you'll have time to think of a way to start a fire on the run back."

For a split second, I had the unmistakable feeling that this was all Emily's fault. Her lizard's curse was hanging over our entire expedition. Then I just started thinking about her and Mum at the deli, with all its pastries, sandwiches, cured meat and glasses of water whenever you wanted them. Almost crying, I scooped up a handful of dirt with my Wolverine claw.

"Digging the well?" Frankie asked.

"No, our shallow graves."

CHAPTER TWELVE

From the pages of Emily Zipzer's field notebook...

3:43 p.m., 7th May

Papa Pete made friendly gestures early on, yet his later actions show that he has sided with the mother. Although I am not washing up as the mother would have hoped, he has me waiting tables.

I protested. I explained that I should be auditing his accounts, reviewing his stocktaking procedures, looking for holes in his supply chain. These words clearly frightened him.

He disguised his betrayal of me by saying, "Everyone starts somewhere." Then he had the nerve to claim that even the eminent Charles Darwin started out waiting tables. That is not true. Darwin studied at Edinburgh and Cambridge universities before joining the voyage of the *Beagle* at the age of 22.

Papa Pete pretended not to hear me when I told him this. I am beginning to learn that the truth is too frightening for most people. They fear it like they fear an approaching enemy.

I have not given up hope, however. As I still aspire to run this place, I decided to use my time waiting tables to make a study of the customers in their natural environment.

General Impressions: on the whole I find the customers disagreeable. They are listless, flabby, and make decisions that are not in their best interests. This last observation I find the most puzzling.

Example: a morbidly obese adult male was sitting at table seven with his teenage son, a squirrelly boy with extensive acne. The adult male ordered a chocomochaccino with cream, and the teenage male ordered a pannacotta. I determined both orders to be totally irrational.

In a show of decency, I "corrected" their orders, and brought instead a black coffee for the adult male and a plate of carrots for the teenage male. They did not immediately appreciate why my substitutions were superior to their original orders.

I explained to the adult male, very slowly so he could understand, that a chocomochaccino is very high in saturated fats, and that he should avoid it for the sake of his cardiovascular health. He did not understand my words.

I explained, more simply this time, that he needed to lower his cholesterol. And to the teenage male, I explained that fresh veggies would help to clear up his skin.

I was perfectly reasonable and rational, but they saw neither reason nor rationality. The adult male said that he could make his "own decisions".

Certainly he could make his own decisions, I replied, but mine were better. The adult male then reacted emotionally and asked to see my manager.

His emotional reaction I find very interesting. When he was presented with the truth, he attempted to reject it, like Papa Pete. But while Papa Pete pretended not to "hear" the truth, the obese adult male actively resisted it with male pattern violence.

(Throughout the day, I have noticed several similar reactions. I am beginning to formulate a thesis: the masses are not fit to make their own decisions!)

I also suspect Papa Pete has grown suspicious of me. He knows that I have been observing that the deli does not run very smoothly under his management. He worries that I will tell the mother. He watches me writing these observations. He watches, yet can do nothing to stop me.

CHAPTER THIRTEEN

We had been running for hours. We had run
all the way to the ridge on the horizon. We
had found nothing there. And so we had
run back. We had run through mud, through
puddles, through tall grass, through nettles.
We had run for so long that we could
hardly remember what life was like before
we began running. We had pushed through
cramps and pain until we just sort of felt
nothing. We had lost all hope.

Now Frankie and I were running back to
the campsite, where we had no tent, no

latrine, no well, and no dinner waiting.

Before we had left camp, I dug a hole a few feet deep but had to stop when my hand started throbbing and clenched shut. Frankie had rigged up a tool out of sticks and rocks to hook onto the packet of rice and try to rescue it from the stinging nettles. He had to give up when he got stung by a wasp in his armpit. He said he'd never known a pain like that in all his life. Our only hope was that Ashley had returned to the campsite with a suitcase full of contraband – beautiful, lovely contraband.

We were deep in Miss Adolf's world. Back in the real world, Miss Adolf was always on at me for living in my own fantasy world. But at least my fantasy world was harmless and fun. It was full of cool birds, spaceships, banana peels and night-vision goggles. Miss Adolf's fantasy world was a pit of despair, filled only with sweat, weird prodding sticks, mud and—

"Stop! Hank, stop!"

Frankie pulled up and hunched over, gasping for air. I'd never seen Frankie so filthy. He's the clean one. That's his thing.

"Hank, not one more step. Look."

My foot was hovering three inches above a cowpat the size of an extra large pizza. "Phew. That was close."

"Don't look now, but we're surrounded," Frankie said.

We *were* surrounded. On every side, as far as the eye could see, were cowpats. It was a cowpat minefield! There was literally no safe step. Ah yes, we were deep in Miss Adolf's world.

"How long have we been running through this?" I asked.

"I don't know."

"How do we get out of this?"

"I don't know."

"Is your name Frankie?"

"I don't know."

"Frankie, snap out of it, man!"

"I can't take it any more, Hank. It's too disgusting. Miss Adolf is taking me apart, piece by piece."

"We're going to make it, I promise. And when we get back to camp, there'll be food waiting. I'm going to text Ashley and have her bring an enormous pizza on the next minibus. A pizza so big they'll have to strap it to the roof."

I got my phone out from my nether parts. I had seven text messages from Ashley.

1. "Your parents are being weird."

2. "Your parents seem lonely. Keep saying they can't remember how to have fun on their own."

3. "Your mum just made me a sandwich and watched me eat every bite. Said she missed you and Emily 'too much', but you've only been gone a day!"

4. "Your parents are making me play board games."

98

5. "Your mum is braiding my hair. Sez she wants to adopt me. What is going on?"

6. "Your parents are definitely trying to kidnap me. Doors locked. Windows also locked."

7. "Help!"

"Never mind Ashley," I said. "She's abandoned us. I'll just have to get the pizza guy to deliver it here."

Frankie stared at my phone. "Oh. You have a *real* phone. I thought it was just one of your make-believe phones. You can't have that. If Miss Adolf sees it—"

A whistle screamed across the sky. We really were in Miss Adolf's fantasy world. All you had to do was *think* her name and she materialized into the nightmare.

"Henry Zipzerrrrr!" came the approaching voice of the undead.

"Quick," I said, and chucked the phone at Frankie. "Hide it."

"I don't want it," he said, and chucked it

back. But Dad's plastic zip-up bag had made it all slippery, and the phone slipped through my catlike grip ... and fell with a nauseating plop into the middle of a cowpat, splattering Frankie.

With the balance of a ballerina and the agility of a cat, Miss Adolf had flawlessly negotiated the cowpat minefield and was standing in front of us. "What are you two doing?" she asked.

"I thought I saw a ruby," I said.

"And why would you think that?" She poked at the nearest cowpat with her stick.

"Isn't this a treasure-hunting expedition, Miss? I thought I signed up for Treasure-Hunting Camp."

"When the bear began eating the funny one, Henry, the funny one wasn't laughing any more," Miss Adolf said. Then she prodded Frankie's earlobe. "You've soiled yourself, Frankie."

Frankie sighed. He was covered in cow

poo. "I quit. I'm getting the next minibus out of here. You can come with me or not, Hank, but I can't take it any more."

"I'd like to say it was a valiant effort, Frankie," Miss Adolf said. "But it wasn't."

"You can't go, Frankie," I cried. "Who will I camp with now?"

He shrugged, and then, with his head down, Frankie began the long, slow march towards the Quitters' Express.

"Come with me, Henry," Miss Adolf said, and prodded me in the armpit. "I think I can find someone for you to camp with."

CHAPTER FOURTEEN

Miss Adolf prodded me back to the campsite
and over to a perfectly erected tent with a
fire-pit in front. Hanging on vines beside it
were socks, clean T-shirts and a Westbrook
Academy blazer. No one was home, but
it wasn't hard to figure out who my new
partner was.

"McKelty is probably in the woods
foraging for food items. He's an excellent
outdoorsman, and should make you a fine
partner," Miss Adolf said before retiring to her
giant tent on the opposite side of the field.

I brought my gear over to my new tent. Inside, everything was neatly arranged. And by neatly, I mean compulsively. McKelty's sleeping bag was in a perfectly straight line and unzipped just a tad. The unzipped part was folded over like in an advert in a camping brochure.

He had a camping pillow, too, and a footstool. Arranged on top of the stool were all his many toiletries, including hair gel, mouthwash and an economy-size bottle of baby powder.

I don't know why, but the giant bottle of baby powder seriously weirded me out. Hanging from a hook on the tent was a calfskin canteen — three-quarters full. I left him a few sips. OK, one sip.

I lay on top of McKelty's sleeping bag while I went through his rucksack. He was loaded up with survival gear. He also had plenty of sweaters and waterproofs, but, sadly, nothing edible, unless you counted the toothpaste. And I counted the toothpaste. Because I ate it.

Then I laid out my supplies. As I didn't have a sleeping bag, I used the complimentary dental T-shirt as a cover and half of my socks for pillows.

After I'd rested a bit and drank the last of McKelty's water, I placed one of the giant boulders Miss Adolf had made me carry under McKelty's sleeping bag, right where his bum would go. Then I went out to tell him the good news about his new tent-mate.

Our tent was one of only four still standing, including Miss Adolf's. Everyone else had taken the Quitters' Express minibus. It was pretty eerie out. Like a ghost town. The sun was starting to go down, a fog was moving in, and it was getting pretty cold. I went back inside and grabbed one of McKelty's scratchy sweaters.

It took me a while to find him on the campsite. He was crouching by this hedge, holding a thin rope. He wasn't moving at all, and he seemed to be thinking about something very hard.

"What are you doing, partner?" I said, and clapped his shoulder. After lying on his sleeping bag, drinking his water, and rummaging through his stuff, I felt pretty familiar with McKelty. But the rude jerk shushed me.

"I'm hunting," he whispered sharply. "Did you say partner?"

"Looks like you caught a hedge."

"It's a trap. Why did you call me partner?"

"Isn't it obvious? We're bunking together. Miss Adolf's orders. My stuff's all moved in."

"Looks like you helped yourself to *my* stuff." He tried to touch the sweater.

"Hey, that's mine. My dad just bought this for me. You have one like it?"

"Shut up, Hank. I'm trying to hunt. There's a noose at the other end. As soon as a bird wanders in – bang!"

"You got dynamite over there?"

"No!" With great agitation, he ran his fingers through his perfectly groomed blond hair. "I just catch it with the rope. Understand?"

"Not really. You want to eat a bird? Sounds gross."

"You eat chicken, don't you? What do you think that is?"

I shrugged. "Let me hold that for a while."

"No." He yanked the rope away from me. "You don't know how. My dad's been teaching me to live off the land. There's food all around us."

"You're right. I saw half a hedgehog on the road over there."

"That's not what I mean and you know it. You have to connect with your hunter sense. Listen, feel, smell and, most of all, be quiet. I'm going to be the first kid to survive this weekend, because only I've got what it takes."

I stopped talking and let McKelty play at survival hunter. After a few minutes, though, I kind of started to get what he was talking about.

If you slowed down and just observed, you could hear the birds. There was even a pattern to their chirps. They'd respond to one another, or one would fly over to a branch to peck at another bird and fight for space.

There was a lot of stuff going on out in the wild. Bugs crawling. Winds changing. Leaves rattling.

Leaves rattling!

The sound was coming from the trap. I elbowed McKelty. He'd heard it too.

He motioned me to be still. But I couldn't! There was something moving about in our trap, and I grabbed the rope from him and gave it a yank. I had something! I guessed it was a badger from the weird barking moan it made.

I gave the rope another yank and whatever I had fell over with a thud and let out a scratchy dinosaur wail.

"We've got a badger!" I whispered.

We poked our heads over the hedge, and although I didn't see anything, McKelty grabbed my shoulder and told me to run.

I ran.

When you're in the wild and someone tells you to run with fear in his eyes, you run. Even if it's McKelty.

CHAPTER FIFTEEN

**From the pages of Emily Zipzer's field
notebook...**

6:21 p.m., 7th May

As a natural scientist, I must embrace the
cold, hard facts of reality, no matter how
ugly.

   Facts: simply put, I have lost control of
the situation. The customers are rioting.
They are angry, violent, out for blood.
Although I do not understand why, I am the

source of their anger. In short, I do not like the public, and they do not like me.

I am afraid I cannot win the day with reason and rationality. The public do not hold these values in high regard. They value "feelings". I do not understand these feelings.

What I have learned today is that the public are NOT equipped to make their own decisions. Customer after customer made the wrong ordering choice, and that means they are making the wrong life choices. Yet when I tried to correct them, each and every customer resented me for it.

I must keep this entry short. I have retreated to the high ground of the deli counter. I am surrounded. The customers try to grab my feet with their grubby hands. I try to talk reasonably to them, but my reason only angers them further.

All is lost.

Papa Pete has called the mother. She is

on her way. She will restore order.

Hurry up, Mum! Please. They are coming too quickly for me to keep them at bay.

CHAPTER SIXTEEN

"It was Miss Adolf," McKelty was saying. "You lassoed Miss Adolf."

"You keep saying that, but I know in my heart it was a badger. Human beings don't make a sound like that."

"*I* saw it — I mean, her. She was on the ground, in the mud. You lassoed Miss Adolf!"

"Maybe Miss Adolf was just taking a nap? Or maybe Miss Adolf is actually a badger. Like, that's her spirit animal."

"There were no badgers *anywhere* in the picture!" McKelty shouted. "*You* lassoed Miss

Adolf, pure and simple. *You* drank all my vitamin water. *You* are wearing *my* sweater. *You* are the worst tent partner ever."

"I don't know what you're talking about. My dad bought me this sweater."

We were sitting around the fire-pit outside his tent. It turns out that McKelty is pretty good at starting a fire. Personally, I think he's a pyromaniac. He kept calling it "my fire", and his eyes showed a little extra white every time he said the words.

Just then Miss Adolf stalked past us. She was scowling and noticeably limping as she leaned on her prodding stick. Her face and most of her khaki short-suit were streaked with light-brown mud.

OK, so maybe I *had* lassoed Miss Adolf. But the evidence was entirely circumstantial.

I lowered my head and pretended to be busy with the fire. "We're in this together now, McKelty," I muttered.

"Why? *You* lassoed her."

"But it was *your* badger trap."

"Are you trying to blackmail me, Zitzer?"

"That's a nasty thing to say to your partner," I said. I picked up the rice packet and tried to read the instructions.

"*Now* what are you doing?"

I thought that was pretty obvious. "I thought I'd cook the rice," I said. "See? I'm just trying to help."

"And burn it? You're useless. Gimme that." He snatched the bag from me.

I tried to snatch it back, but it flew from both our hands and landed in the fire. It started burning immediately ... and smelling terrible.

"Get it out!" McKelty cried.

I grabbed a long poking stick and hooked the rice out of the fire. The bag was still burning, though. It set fire to the stick. I swung it about to try and put out the flames and − accidentally − sent it on a collision course with McKelty's face and beautiful hair. He judo-chopped the stick, sending it flying out of my hands and onto the tent. That started burning too.

Thinking fast, I tore off the jumper and used it to pat down the smoldering tent.

McKelty glared at me as he picked up the jumper. The tag sticking out of it was clearly labelled "Property of Nick McKelty".

CHAPTER SEVENTEEN

McKelty had a very long, very involved and very secretive night-time grooming routine. He did a hundred jumping jacks. He flossed. He combed his hair. He applied moisturizers. He relaced his shoes. Exactly seven times. He did a lot of things exactly seven times.

Just when I was starting to think that maybe, just maybe, McKelty and I had more in common than I'd thought, he left the tent for several minutes with his jumbo bottle of baby powder to finish "washing up". The imagination reeled.

I covered the hole in the tent with my worst pair of underwear. It was right over where McKelty's right knee would go when he was in his sleeping bag.

Although I was bone-tired, I couldn't sleep. I had no blankets, no bedding, and the tent smelled like molten plastic, McKelty's toiletries, cowpats and, once McKelty had returned, baby powder.

"I'm so hungry," McKelty said as he got into his sleeping bag. He somehow managed to avoid lying on the boulder I'd left for him.

"Have one of my sucking stones," I said.

"What?"

"Suck on a rock. It helps with hunger."

I gave him a little pebble the size of my fingertip.

He examined it. "Have you sucked on this one?"

"No."

"How do you know?"

"I've got a system. The ones in my right

117

pocket are fresh, the ones in my left pocket have already been sucked."

"All right, I guess." Beneath the sound of the tent canvas flapping in the night breeze, I could hear the sucking stone knocking against his teeth. "It does help."

"Or was it the left pocket...?"

"Ugh." He chucked the stone at the roof of the tent and noticed my underpants hanging there, covering the patch. "Why would you use underpants?"

"Fixed the hole, didn't I?"

"You could have used almost anything else, but you used your underpants."

"They're cleanish."

"But just looking at them makes the tent smell worse."

"You're all riled up, McSmelty. Want me to teach you my deep breathing exercises?"

"I want to swap places with you. I can't look at those pants one second longer."

"Can I use your camping mat?"

"Fine. Just—" He swung his sleeping-bagged legs over mine to try to hoist himself over me and swap places. He wound up falling on my hip bone. *"Owwww."*

"Shut up," I said. "Do you hear that?"

"It's my back breaking, you idiot."

"No, listen."

We listened. Some sort of creature was coming closer, rustling leaves and breaking branches while making a guttural breathing and clicking sound. For a moment, it stopped and there was silence. Then there was this low, rumbling growl that seemed to slide inside the tent and poke my heart.

"It's right outside," McKelty whispered, and turned off his torch.

"It's the badger, I know it."

"What does it want?"

"Our food."

"We burned the rice." McKelty buried his head in his sleeping bag. "Go away," he muttered. "Leave us alone."

"It's OK. I have something..."

I pulled the cake mix from my rucksack.

"Urggg, what's that smell?" McKelty cried.

"Special camping food," I said. "Military-issue stuff."

I chucked the tub of cake mix through the hole in the tent and then quickly plugged it back up with my undies and McKelty's charred sweater. The creature outside seemed to groan *thank you*. Then there was the sound of paws clicking on plastic as it scampered away.

We lay without talking for a while. I listened to McKelty breathing loudly through his mouth and tried not to notice the baby powder aroma in my nostrils. Just as my eyes were finally shutting, a whistle pierced the night.

"Attention! Attention!" It was Miss Adolf. "The last minibus is leaving in ten minutes! All quitters prepare yourselves. This will

be the last minibus of the night. Leave now, or face more unknowns of the dark! That is all."

It was obvious the people in the other tents were packing it in.

"I'll go if you go," McKelty said in a very small voice.

"Never."

Soon we heard the minibus rev its engine as it headed towards freedom and plenty. Then everything was quiet again. I fell asleep to the sound of McKelty whimpering. That could have been me, however. Nah, it was definitely McKelty.

CHAPTER EIGHTEEN

A horrible groaning wail broke into my dreams and woke me in the dark night and the talcum aroma of the tent. It was the sound of sheer agony.

First thought: aliens! Second thought: some sort of mammal-sized insect is being digested alive.

"Mama, what is that?" McKelty said and sat bolt upright. He saw me, slapped himself, as he remembered where he was, and tried to act cool. "It isn't one of the other campers. Everyone's gone."

"That's not human."

The wail came again, this time with a rumbling gurgle that I felt in my ribcage.

"Yes, it is," McKelty said. "And it needs our help."

The next cry came, rapid fire, followed by the most dreadful moaning. And then, weakly, trickling through the inky night, came the words *"Heeeeelp meeeeeee..."*

It was Miss Adolf.

"We're coming, Miss!" McKelty shouted and dragged me into the night.

The sound was definitely coming from Miss Adolf's giant tent. A light was on in there.

"Maybe she's mutating?" I suggested.

"What?"

"Yeah," I said. "Maybe she's mutating into her spirit animal."

"Don't be an idiot," McKelty said, running across the field and creeping up to the open flap of the tent. "But there may be an

123

animal in there, so be ready to fight it off. On three. Ready?"

"No."

"One, two…"

"Tonobungay!" I shouted, and jumped inside the tent, hands out, ready to pounce.

A horrid wall of smell stopped me in my tracks and made me weak in the knees. I looked around.

On a table there was an iPod playing "Haunted Sounds of the Woods". Yet the music wasn't playing any more, and the rumbling sound was still rumbling.

I scanned the tent to the bed. There was Miss Adolf, lying on her back, her stomach shaking. Her head was rolled back and her tongue was hanging out. She started pointing at her gurgling stomach and shaking her head. *No… No…*

Then she rolled over, opened her mouth and threw up. I'll say no more about it. It's bad enough remembering it.

"Food poisoning," she groaned. "Call ... an ... ambulance."

"Right away, Miss," McKelty said. "Where's a phone?"

"All gone... Sent them back on the ... minibus. Oooohhhaaaaahgggggguurr."

That was when I noticed my tub of cake mix on the floor next to Miss Adolf's camp bed. It was open. Some creature, maybe the badger, had eaten at least half of it. Or maybe...

"Did you eat *this*?" I asked Miss Adolf.

When she caught sight of the tub, her eyes rolled back in her head. She pointed at her stomach and groaned. "Get that ... away! Oooooh!"

Miss Adolf puked a second time.

McKelty pulled me to one side. Miss Adolf had rolled into a ball and was starting to shiver.

"What are we going to do?" he asked.

"AHHHHHHHH!" Miss Adolf screamed.

"I have a phone," I said. Then my own stomach heaved as I remembered where it was. "Oh no. No. Noooooooo."

CHAPTER NINETEEN

If you are reading this, I consider you my
friend. So for the sake of our friendship, I
won't tell you everything that happened
over that next hour or so. I will only tell you
what you need to know. But nothing more.

Nothing more.

You know already that McKelty and I
crawled on our hands and knees through the
cowpat minefield, poking and prodding at
no less than five hundred individual pizza-
sized cow deposits, looking for the stupid
plastic bag that contained my mobile phone.

You know that it was freezing. You know that an animal was tracking us the entire time, drawing nearer. You also know that it started raining. And you know that I puked up my orange juice.

What you don't know is that my aim was less than stellar. Aside from my fingers, a little of the — shall we say "recoil"? — splashed my partner. And my partner promptly threw up himself, breaking seven generations of McKelty family tradition — "McKeltys don't puke" — and I got to know him from the inside-out.

Let me skip over the next few minutes. All I will say is that we spent them letting the beautiful, cleansing rain wash over us.

I don't know who found the phone at last, or where. It was under a rain-soaked cowpat that looked like every other rain-soaked cowpat. I'm almost certain I found it, but McKelty and I were like a creature of one flesh by then.

I had five texts from Frankie:

1. "Something weird is going on in your house. Parents are all nice."

2. "Your parents have gone mental. Won't let Ash or me leave. Never want to stop playing Snakes and Ladders."

3. "Parents are kidnapping us. All doors and windows locked!"

4. "Ash has Stockholm syndrome. Thinks she's Emily. Wearing her glasses. Petting Katherine. Calling your parents 'Mum' and 'Dad'."

5. "Looks like I'm adopted too!"

I called Frankie to send help. I called Ashley. I called my parents. No one responded. It was the middle of the night. No one was coming.

Through the wind and the rain, I heard the distant call of a badger puking up on an empty stomach.

McKelty and I put our heads down and ran back through the rain. But with all the rain, and the barfing, and the hunger, and the adrenaline, and, of course, the cowpat fumes, we couldn't find the campsite, let alone make it out of the cowpat minefield.

"We're going round in circles!" McKelty cried. He dropped to his knees. "Try to use your phone's map. It's our only hope."

Bad idea. The last time I tried to use the Satnav, I got on a slow bus heading for Essex. Like I said, I'm not good with maps.

Instead, I looked through the rain for a familiar landmark. All I saw was rain and muddy fields and the dark night.

You won't believe what happened next. I don't believe it myself. But it really did happen. If you don't believe me, ask McKelty.

Just when I had lost all hope, and was about to plop down in the muddy field next to McKelty and wait for the animal who had been stalking us to eat us alive, it occurred to me that I hadn't heard its call in a while.

And just when I realized that, a flash of lightning split open the sky. In that one-second flicker of light, I saw a small orange shape ahead of us. An animal ... with a crooked white moustache.

It was my old buddy, Alnor the Orange! He must have slipped off the minibus before it left for the night.

Lightning flashed right over our heads. Thunder exploded.

"We're lost for ever," McKelty wailed.

"No, we're not. Follow Alnor! My spirit animal will show us the way. Come on, Alnor, lead us back to camp!"

Alnor looked at me again, then sprang on ahead. I followed, and McKelty had no choice but to run after us.

As soon as we arrived back at camp, McKelty dashed into Miss Adolf's tent, holding my phone.

"It's OK, Miss. I'll save you," he said.

I went over and patted Miss Adolf on the shoulder, leaving a very interesting hand print.

"What's that smell?" she moaned.

"Fresh air, Miss," I said.

She made the dentist-suction-tube sound again and passed out. Her stomach continued to vibrate, though.

Meanwhile, McKelty was on the phone with the authorities. "We need an ambulance! Where are we? Um ... we're—"

I grabbed the phone out of his hand. In my mind, I saw my landmark map. *Bridge ... brownish tree ... waterslide park ... golf course...*

The operator had no trouble translating my map and sent an ambulance right away. While McKelty stayed with Miss Adolf and wiped her brow and massaged her feet, I went out into the night with a torch and Alnor. We waited by the side of the road for the ambulance.

All the paramedics called me a hero. One even gave me a surgical mask to wear. As they were carting off poor Miss Adolf on a stretcher, she briefly came to, caught a hold of McKelty's arm and whispered to him, "Smuggling in a phone. Cheating... You failed..."

McKelty protested, but it was no use: Adolf was out cold.

"I'LL GET YOU FOR THIS, ZITZEEERRRRRRRR!" he cried.

CHAPTER TWENTY

Dad came and got me from the hospital, where my paramedic friend, Omraam, had been nice enough to find me a shower, a clean pair of junior-sized scrubs and five pairs of surgical gloves, just for fun.

Omraam also asked if Alnor could come home with him, since his latest cat, Harley, had just kicked the bucket. Considering the likely carnage of a cat-iguana household, I bid adieu to my little orange friend with the white moustache, and went off with my dad in his car.

We headed to a nearby cafe for a well-deserved breakfast of pancakes and sausage with a side of bacon, and polished it off with a tall glass of orange juice.

"Here's the hero," my mum cried as I came into the flat later that morning and threw myself onto the sofa. "You passed Survival Camp!"

"No, not exactly."

"As far as we're concerned you passed," my dad said. "With flying colours."

"You can go off with your friends whenever you want. And maybe we were being a bit over... We just missed you. We missed *both* of you too much! You have no idea how lonely we've been without you."

My mum squeezed a blanket-covered shape in the corner of the sofa. Glasses poked out of it, along with two yellow lizard's eyes.

"I'm not going anywhere," I said. "Ever again. Have you seen what's out there?" I shivered as I remembered the wailing beast and the thunder and ... the cowpats. "The world's a dangerous place. I'm staying here for at least two weeks."

"Come on, Hank," my dad said. "Shopping's hardly survival camping..."

"It's worse," Emily said, emerging from her blanket cocoon to stroke Katherine. "Believe me, Hank. I've seen what the public are like. They're monsters! I'm staying here with you and my little Katherine... Yes ... what a sweetie face..." And she started making nauseating kissy-kissy noises.

"Well," my mum said, "anyone want to play a board game?"

"I'm in," I said.

"Me too," Emily said.

"Great," said my dad. "Hank, would you care to microwave us a bag of popcorn?"

"I'm your man," I said, and set the microwave for "charred".

the world's **GREATEST** underachiever

HankZIPZER

**Hank is playing the King of Siam in the school play,
but a costume disaster on opening night threatens
the whole show. Can best friends Frankie and
Ashley save the day?**

HankZIPZER

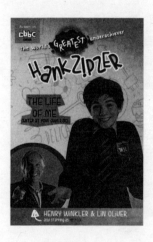

Hank is writing his autobiography for Mr Rock (best teacher ever!) and has a crush on a cute girl called Zoe. Life is good ... until Hank finds out that Zoe is the cousin of his nemesis, McKelty.

HANK ZIPZER

**When Hank enters his dog in a show, he hopes to win
the big prize. Unfortunately, his sister, Emily, has
also entered with her creepy pet iguana.
May the best tail win!**

HankZipZER

Hank's mum is pregnant. How could she do this to him? One annoying sibling is enough. Hank definitely did not order this baby!